Thumbs Up, Rico!

MARIA TESTA

illustrated by
DIANE PATERSON

Albert Whitman & Company, Morton Grove, Illinois

To the Wampanoag Warriors
of the Rhode Island Special Olympics. MT

For my husband, John. DP

Library of Congress Cataloging-in-Publication Data
Testa, Maria.
Thumbs up, Rico! / Maria Testa ; illustrated by Diane Paterson.

p.   cm.

Summary: In three separate stories, a boy with Down syndrome
makes a new friend, helps his sister with a difficult decision,
and finally draws a picture he likes.
ISBN 0-8075-7906-8
1. Children's stories, American. [1. Down syndrome—Fiction.
2. Mentally handicapped—Fiction. 3. Brothers and sisters—Fiction.]
I. Paterson, Diane, ill. II. Title.
PZ7.T2877Th 1994
[E]—dc20   93-29801
                                                           CIP
                                                           AC

Design by Lucy Smith.

Text copyright © 1994 by Maria Testa.
Illustrations copyright © 1994 by Diane Paterson.
Published in 1994 by Albert Whitman & Company,
6340 Oakton Street, Morton Grove, Illinois 60053-2723.
Published simultaneously in Canada
by General Publishing, Limited, Toronto.

Printed in the United States of America.
10 9 8 7 6 5 4 3 2 1

Table of Contents

The First Time I Met Caesar

The first time I met Caesar, he was playing basketball down at the playground. I really wanted to like him. I wanted to like him a lot. But the first time I met Caesar, I didn't like him at all.

Caesar was shooting baskets, one after the other. I wanted to play with him.

"Hi, buddy," I said. "What's your name?"

"Caesar," he said. "And I'm not your buddy. Get out of here, dummy!"

I don't like it when people call me dummy.

"My name's not Dummy," I said. "It's Rico."

Caesar threw the ball at me. He threw it really hard. I could have caught it, only I wasn't ready.

So I dropped it.

"Ha, ha." Caesar pointed at me. "See? You can't even catch a basketball. You *are* a dummy!"

"No, I'm not!" I shouted. But I couldn't think of anything else to say.

I really hate that dummy stuff! And Caesar called me a dummy twice. I stuck my hands in my pockets and walked home.

My sister, Nina, was sitting at the kitchen table having milk and cookies.

"Want a cookie?" she asked.

But I was too sad and angry to eat a cookie. "I met a new boy at the playground," I told Nina. "His name's Caesar. He's a good basketball player."

"Really?" Nina said. "Is he nice?"

I shook my head. "I don't like him. He called me a dummy."

Nina jumped out of her chair and clenched her fists. "Ooh! That makes me sooo mad! Want me to beat him up for you?"

Nina's only one year older than me, but she's a lot bigger. I'm kind of short because I have Down syndrome. She's always asking me if I want her to beat someone up for me. But I never do.

"No," I said to Nina. "Don't beat him up. I want to play basketball with him."

"But you said you don't like him," Nina said. "He called you a dummy! Why would you want to play with him?"

I shrugged my shoulders. "I just like the way he plays basketball."

Suddenly, I had an idea.

"Listen, Nina! Maybe if I get to know him better, I might like him. And maybe if he gets to know *me* better, he won't call me a dummy

anymore. Then he might like me, too. That
would be great!"

Nina frowned. But then she stopped frowning
and stretched her arms out wide.

"Everybody who knows you loves you," she
said. "And don't forget, I know you best of all!"

I stuck my thumb in the air. "Yes!" I shouted.
And I gave her a *big* hug.

The next time I met Caesar, I was bike riding with Nina. Caesar was riding his bike, too.

"Hi, buddy!" I called out to him.

"I'm not your buddy," Caesar said. He didn't call me a dummy. But I think that was because Nina was shaking her fist at him. I still didn't like him very much.

The next time I met Caesar, I was in the mall with my mother. Caesar was there with his father.

"Hi, buddy!" I said to him.

"Hi, Rico," Caesar said. His father said hi, too, and held out his hand. I shook it.

After they left, I turned to my mother and stuck my thumb in the air. "Caesar called me Rico! Yes!"

The next time I met Caesar, I was down at the playground playing basketball with Nina. I was practicing my three-point shot. It was fantastic.

I couldn't miss!

"Look who's here," Nina said.

Caesar was standing at the other end of the court. He was watching us play.

"Hi, buddy!" I called to him. "Want to play with us?"

"Can't," Caesar said. "I have to go home."

He started to walk away. Then he stopped and turned around.

"Hey, Rico!" he called. "You want to play tomorrow?"

"Great!" I pumped my fist. Caesar smiled and waved good-bye.

I stuck my thumb in the air and looked at Nina.

"Yes!" we both shouted.

The next time I met Caesar, it was the next day, down at the playground. Caesar was practicing free throws.

"Hi, buddy!" I said. "My coach says you should bend your knees when you take a free throw."

Caesar looked surprised. "Coach? You play on a team?"

"Sure!" I said. "Don't you?"

Caesar shook his head. "No. But I want to.

Do you think maybe I could play on your team?"

"My team is only for kids with special needs,"
I explained. "I have a big game tomorrow. Want
to come?"

Caesar bent his knees and shot a free throw.
SWISH! Nothing but net.

"Well. . . ," he said, "I think I can make it. It
might be fun."

I held out my hands, and Caesar passed the
ball to me. I drove in for a lay-up. "Yes!" I

shouted, as the ball went through the hoop.

We had a *great* time.

The next time I met Caesar was at my house. He'd come over, and he was watching Nina make a banner for my basketball game. I was already in my uniform, doing my stretching exercises. Nina held up the banner so I could see how cool her printing was.

WAY TO GO, RICO ! !

I laughed. "Hey! You made a rhyme!"

There were a lot of people at the game. The gym was packed. My whole team was super-excited. We had practiced really hard for weeks. If we won this game, we'd be in first place!

We got in our positions for the opening tip-off. The referee tossed the ball into the air. Our center jumped up high and tapped the ball right

to me. I turned to our basket. Wide open! I held the ball over my head to shoot. Suddenly, someone bumped into me. I dropped the ball and heard a whistle. Foul!

I took my place at the foul line, ready to take two free throws. I bent my knees and shot the ball. Good! The crowd cheered, and I looked up into the stands. There was Nina's banner! Caesar was helping Nina hold it up. It was the biggest banner of all!

"WAY TO GO, RICO! !" I read out loud.

But wait! There was a new line on the banner. Caesar was pointing to it.

The new line was the best I ever read:

HI, BUDDY ! !

I shot the second free throw. SWISH! I ran down the court and stuck *both* thumbs in the air.

YES ! !

❖

something for *her*.

I was in the kitchen helping Dad make dinner when the telephone rang. It stopped after two rings.

"Nina must have picked it up," Dad said.

After a minute, Nina charged into the kitchen.

"Sarah Ferguson just invited me to her birthday party!" she shouted. "It's a sleepover, and it's next Saturday. Her parents will be there the whole time. Can I go, Dad? Please, can I go?" Nina was talking really fast. She grabbed Dad's hand and jumped up and down.

Dad laughed. Then he started to jump up and down, too!

"Of course you can go, Nina," he said. "It sounds like fun."

I grabbed Dad's other hand and started jumping with them. We were all laughing really hard, until suddenly I remembered something.

I stopped jumping.

"Wait, Nina," I said. "You can't go to that party."

Nina stopped laughing. "What do you mean, Rico? Why can't I?"

"Saturday's the day of my big basketball playoff," I reminded her. "You can't miss that!"

"I forgot," Nina whispered. "Dad," she said, "what should I do?"

Dad held our hands tightly.

"It's up to you, honey," he said softly. "I think it's your decision."

Nina bit her lip. She looked at me, then at Dad, then back at me again. What was she waiting for?

"Nina!" I cried. "You *have* to come to my game!"

"No, I don't!" she shouted. "I don't have to do anything!" She ran out of the kitchen. I heard

her feet pounding up the stairs.

I was so mad at Nina, I thought I was going to explode. I think she was pretty mad at me, too.

"Are you coming to my game?" I asked her the next morning.

"Don't rush me, Rico," Nina answered. "I haven't decided yet." She picked up her books and ran out to the bus stop without me.

At lunchtime, I saw Nina in the cafeteria at school. She was sitting with a bunch of her friends.

"Are you coming to my game?" I asked her again.

"Stop being such a pain, Rico," she said. "I'll tell you when I decide." Then she started talking to her friends again and ignored me.

After school, Nina was doing her homework at the kitchen table.

"Are you coming to my game?" I asked. Nina

slammed her pencil down on the table.

"Rico, you're driving me crazy!" she shouted.
"I told you I'd let you know when I decide. Can't
you just leave me alone?"

So now I was driving her crazy. Good. I
decided that I would never talk to Nina again for
the rest of my life if she didn't come to my
basketball game.

When the telephone rang, I ran to answer it,
but Nina beat me to it. It was for her, anyway.
I pretended to leave the kitchen, but I waited
around the corner. I didn't want Nina to know
I was listening.

"I'm sorry, Sarah," I heard her say. "I really
want to go to your party, but I want to go to my
brother's game, too." She stopped for a moment.
She was listening to Sarah. "Okay," Nina
continued, "I'll make up my mind tonight. I'll
tell you in school tomorrow."

I tried to get out of the way, but Nina hung up the phone too fast. She caught me standing there. She just stared at me. Then she ran upstairs. I heard her bedroom door slam.

I tiptoed up the stairs and stopped at Nina's room. I stood right by the door and listened hard.

Nina was crying. She cried for a long time. Why was she so sad? Did I make her cry?

I touched my face. My cheeks were wet. Ever since I was a little baby, I've always cried when Nina cries. That's because I love her so much. And I

23

know how much she loves me, too. I wasn't mad anymore.

I stood outside her bedroom and remembered when I was little. I thought about growing up with Nina, the best sister in the world. I thought about how much she always did for me. And I knew that now I could finally do something for Nina.

I knocked on her door. "Nina," I called.

"Please open the door."

After a moment, the door opened. Nina's eyes were red. I knew mine were, too.

"I'm sorry," I said.

Nina smiled a little. "So am I."

I held my arms out wide, and Nina hugged me. It was a great big hug. Nina's hugs are the best.

"Nina," I whispered into her ear, "I want you to go to the party. I want you to have a great time."

"Do you really, Rico?" she asked. "Are you sure?"

"I'm sure," I said, and I hugged her even tighter.

My sister smiled. "Thank you," she said. "You don't know how much this means to me."

I smiled, too, but I didn't say anything.

Yes I do, Nina. Yes I do.

❖

I'm pretty good at a lot of things. I'm a good basketball player. I'm a really good friend. And I'm a *great* brother. But one thing I'm not good at is art. Art is my worst subject at school.

"I know I'm not very good at art," I told Ms. Jefferson, "but you're my favorite teacher anyway." Ms. Jefferson is the best art teacher I've ever had. She lets us have a lot of fun in class, even if we make a mess.

"I'm glad I'm your favorite teacher, Rico," she said. "But I think that you *are* good at art."

"All of my drawings are terrible!" I said. "They're never good enough to hang on the bulletin board." Every week, Ms. Jefferson asks the kids to hang their favorite drawings on the bulletin board. But I never do because I don't like any of my drawings.

"Do you know what I think, Rico?" Ms. Jefferson asked. "I think you'd like your drawings a lot more if you drew something that really interests you. Do you agree?"

"You bet, Ms. Jefferson," I said. "I think so, too."

On Monday, after school, I sat at the kitchen table with a sheet of paper and a box of crayons in front of me. Mom and Dad were sitting with me. They were paying the bills. I was trying to think of something that interested me.

"What should I draw?" I asked.

"Why don't you pretend we're rich," Mom said, "and draw a big, beautiful mansion for us to live in."

"Great!" I said. "That's interesting." So

that's what I decided to do.

But something was wrong. I had never seen a mansion. I didn't know what one looked like.

I started the drawing lots of times, but I kept getting stuck. Finally, I drew a big house and colored it with different crayons. But when I finished, it just looked like one thing. Mud.

On Friday, a lot of kids hung their drawings on the bulletin board. I hid my muddy mansion inside my desk.

Sammy hung up his drawing of a sailboat. It was really good.

"That's a great sailboat, Sammy," I said.

"Thanks, Rico," Sammy said. "Where's your drawing?"

"I didn't hang one up this week," I explained. "But I will next week."

I hoped I was telling the truth.

The next Monday, after school, I was at Caesar's house. We were trading baseball cards.

"What should I do for my next drawing, Caesar?" I asked.

Caesar held up a baseball card.

"Why don't you draw a baseball field," he said. "That should be easy. It's shaped like a diamond."

"That's a good idea," I said. So that's what I decided to do.

But when I sat down to draw, something was wrong. I drew a diamond, but it didn't look like a baseball field. I colored it green, but the green didn't look like grass. And I made a real mess of the pitcher's mound.

When I held up the drawing, it looked like just one thing. Mud again. Only this time, the mud looked kind of green.

On Friday, I stuffed my muddy-green baseball field deep inside my backpack. I didn't want to hang it on the bulletin board.

Marta's drawing of her dog was on the board. It was very good, especially the eyes.

"Your dog looks great, Marta," I said.

"Thanks, Rico," Marta said. "Next week, you should hang one of your drawings on the bulletin board, too."

"I will, Marta," I said. But I wasn't so sure.

The next Monday, after school, I was playing in the backyard with Nina. We were making paper airplanes.

"I have to do another drawing this week," I told Nina. "What should I do?"

Nina tossed a paper plane into the air.

"I know," she said. "You should draw a big plane, like a 747, flying above the clouds."

"That's a great idea, Nina," I said. "That's really interesting. That's what I'm going to do."

I worked hard on that drawing. I even tried to

copy a picture
of a jet plane
from my science
book. But nothing I
drew looked like an
airplane, no matter how hard
I tried. Every time I made a
mistake, I crumpled the paper into a ball and
threw it across the kitchen.

Finally, I got tired of all the mistakes.

"No!" I shouted. I picked up the crumpled
balls and threw them everywhere. "No, no, no!"

Dad rushed into the kitchen. He stopped
when he saw what I had done.

"I draw like a baby!" I cried. "I hate art!"

"Right now," Dad said, "you're acting like a
baby, too."

He picked up one of my drawings and
smoothed it out.

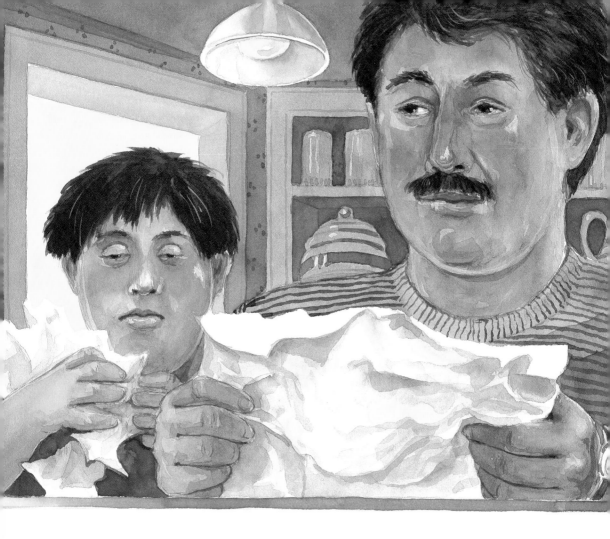

"This is a good drawing, Rico," he said.
"Much better than you used to do."

I didn't know what to say. I started to clean
up the mess. Dad didn't say anything else either.
He helped me pick up all the crumpled drawings.

I felt bad about the way I acted. But I still hated art.

On Friday, I didn't even look at the bulletin board.

Last Monday, after school, I picked up my basketball and went down to the playground. I needed to think.

I took a foul shot. SWISH! That was easy.

I took a lay-up. SWISH! That was easy, too.

I took a three-pointer. SWISH! Even that was pretty easy.

Then I thought about the drawing I had to do that week. It would be hard. I had already asked my parents, Caesar, and Nina for ideas about what to draw. I didn't know who to ask next.

I practiced my dribbling and thought about the drawing.

I practiced my jump shot and thought about the drawing.

I practiced my hook shot and thought about the drawing.

I wished I was taller. If I was taller, I bet I could even slam dunk.

Then it hit me. I didn't have to ask anybody for an idea about what to draw. I had my own idea. It was a really good one, too.

Suddenly, I knew I could do the best drawing of my life.

On Friday, I got to school early. I wanted to be the first to hang a drawing on the bulletin board.

Sammy came in next. He looked at my drawing. "Wow!" he said. "That is so cool, Rico."

Then Marta came in. "Great drawing, Rico!" she said.

Pretty soon, the whole class was standing in front of the bulletin board. Ms. Jefferson walked into the room.

"Good morning, everyone," she said. "What are you all looking at?" She went over to the bulletin board, too.

Then she saw it. In the very center of the

bulletin board, there was a drawing of a boy soaring high into the air, about to stuff a basketball through a hoop. That boy was me. And that was *my* slam dunk.

Ms. Jefferson smiled. "Congratulations, Rico!" she said. "I knew you could do it. That is a fantastic drawing."

"It's just a dream," I explained. "I could never really slam dunk."

Ms. Jefferson raised her eyebrows. We looked at my drawing, and then we both smiled.

"But who knows?" I said. "Maybe someday I will!"